THIS Picture Knight BOOK
BELONGS TO

.................,.....................

The Adventures of Maurice Mini Minor

GEOFFREY BAKER

Maurice breathes again

illustrated by *Rolf Harris*

Picture Knight

HODDER AND STOUGHTON

With thanks to the members of the
Maidenhead Static Model Club
for kind assistance

From an original idea by Dr P. Mansfield and Terry Moule

British Library Cataloguing in Publication Data

Baker, Geoffrey
Maurice breathes again.
I. Title   II. Harris, Rolf, *1930-*   III. Series
823'.914 [J]

ISBN 0-340-52959-8

First published 1990 by Picture Knight

Published by Hodder and Stoughton Children's Books,
a division of Hodder and Stoughton Ltd,
Mill Road, Dunton Green, Sevenoaks, Kent TN13 2YA
Editorial office: 47 Bedford Square, London WC1E 7DP

Printed in Great Britain by Cambus Litho, East Kilbride

'Remember we have to go through the Very Long Tunnel soon,' shouted Maurice Mini Minor. He had to shout because Sir Reginald Hoy-Titoyty and Cheeky Beetle and Mam'selle Mimi were driving along with him on their way to the seaside.

'I've dropped my bucket and spade,' yelled Cheeky Beetle.

'No jokes today, please,' shouted Maurice, 'and certainly not while we're driving on a main road.'

'Here, here,' thundered Sir Reginald.

When they arrived at the Very Long Tunnel, Mimi called out, 'Remember it's always full of exhaust fumes. They make you feel terribly tired and sick if you're in there too long. Don't stop.'

'Exactly,' shouted Maurice, 'a nice gentle pace so that you don't suck in too many fumes.'

They drove into the tunnel. The light got yellower and the air got greyer.

'Who's that?' yelled Mimi suddenly.

Ahead of them, someone had stopped on the side of the road.

'It's Mr and Mrs Splicer,' shouted Cheeky Beetle. 'They must be going to the seaside too. Slow down and see if we can help!'

What a sorry sight! The Splicers had totally broken down. Their engine was wheezing deeply and was far too weak to move them.

'Exploding exhaust pipes,' exclaimed Maurice, 'they've sucked in too many fumes. Quickly; we'll have to get them out before the same thing happens to us. Sir Reginald, you push from behind, you're the strongest.'

'Feeling a bit croaky myself actually,' coughed Sir Reginald, 'but I'll try.' He managed to push the Splicers a little way forward but then *he* stopped. 'I need a rest,' he mumbled.

'Keep going,' shouted Maurice hoarsely but in vain. Already, he could feel the fumes creeping into his own carburettor and slowing *his* engine down. Quickly he hooked his bumper onto the Splicers' side car and pulled, but all his energy had drained away. 'I need a rest,' he muttered.

'What shall we do?' yelled Cheeky Beetle.
'I'll get help if I can,' choked Mimi and she
spluttered off down the tunnel.

Cheeky Beetle stared through the fumes at all his friends. He felt lonely and frightened and very weak too.

Then, suddenly, he had a very cheeky idea and with all the energy he had left, he screamed, 'Look out! The Red Rusty Monster is coming down the tunnel with bits flaking off him and holes in his sides and spots all over him and jagged teeth that are going to eat you up and...'

Cheeky didn't need to scream any more. They *all* jumped forward in fright and coughed and jerked and spluttered down the tunnel and out into the open air.

'What happened?' cried Mimi who was standing on the roadside getting her breath back. A loud bang came from the Splicers' exhaust pipe which made them all jump again.

'Ah well,' puffed Sir Reginald, 'there was this . . . er . . . there was . . . a . . .'

'A WHAT?' shouted Mimi.

'It was . . . er . . .' said Mr Splicer, 'it was . . . a . . .'

'Bad dream?' suggested Mrs Splicer.

'Bad dream,' said her husband.

'A monstrous dream,' Cheeky Beetle said with a grin.

Maurice managed a smile. 'Come on,' he said, 'let's have a nice dream at the seaside. We're nearly there now.'

And so they were. Soon the fresh air blew round their engines and they felt wonderful again.

'Let's drive onto the pier,' Maurice yelled.

They did, and stared at the waves crashing below them.

'I feel a new car,' boomed Sir Reginald.

'Yes,' said Maurice. 'It's what we all need; big gulps of fresh air. That's why I go for a quick drive every morning. Once we get clogged up with smoke or fumes, nothing works properly any more and you know what happens then.'

'We certainly do,' they all said.

'Let's go home by the other road,' suggested Cheeky Beetle. 'It will take more time, but we won't have to go through the Very Long Tunnel at all.'

'Splendid idea,' thundered Sir Reginald.

'That's not the only splendid idea Cheeky Beetle has had today, is it?' said Maurice. They all looked rather sheepishly at him.

'Yes,' said Maurice, 'that was a clever and very monstrous joke to play on us, Cheeky. Well done.'

'Look out!' Cheeky Beetle yelled. 'There's a huge wave coming.'

Of course, nobody believed him but it was true! The wave crashed against the pier and drenched them all with spray.

'Good old Cheeky,' they laughed and Maurice sang a little song.

MAURICE'S SONG

Down in the tunnel, the air was thick,
Exhaust fumes swirling and grey;
The Splicers stopped, air filters blocked,
It wasn't their best fun day.
'How lucky,' we thought, when we arrived,
But the fumes made us all choke;
It was Cheeky who saved the day at last
With a marvellous monstrous joke.
'Well done,' we cried, 'for getting us out,'
And Sir Reginald coughed, 'Here, here!'
Then we breathed fresh air down by the sea,
(*And* got drenched by a wave on the pier.)

So
Every morning clean your teeth,
And brush your straggly hair;
Find your clothes – there they are,
Scattered everywhere!

Go to the window – open it up,
Take great gulps of air,
Fill your lungs, puff out your chest,
And sing this if you dare:

I'm clean as a whistle, sharp as a thistle,
Strong as a lion or an ox; (deep breath)
Bright as a button, tough as old mutton,
Fresh as a daisy not smelly old socks.
No fuming, no choking, no croaking, no
  smoking,
Breathe as deep as a well, (deep breath)
No fuming, no choking, no croaking, no
  smoking,
Sing as clear as a bell (deep breath).

I sing this song as I drive along,
Maurice Mini Minor;
I get there soon 'cause I keep in tune,
Maurice Mini Minor;
And when you see me passing by,
Just toot your horn and wink your eye,
No need to wonder who am I,
Maurice Mini Minor.